Hotwife's Hidden Desires: Watching My Wife Book Two

Hotwife's Hidden Desires, Volume 2

Karly Violet

Published by Karly Violet, 2020.

HOTWIFE'S HIDDEN DESIRES: WATCHING MY WIFE BOOK TWO

First edition. April 13, 2020.

ISBN: 978-1393520504

Written by Karly Violet.

Hotwife's Hidden Desires: Watching My Wife

A Wife Sharing Multiple Partner Romance Novel

Author's note: All character in this story are 18 years of age and older. This is a work of fiction, any resemblance to real live name or events are purely coincidental.

Be aware: This story is written for, and should only be enjoyed by, ADULTS. It includes explicit descriptions of intense sexual activity between consenting adults.

Note that this work of fiction resembles a fantasy world, all events taking place are a result of a role play amongst all parties and all parties are fully consenting adults.

This ebook should be purchased/borrowed by and read by adults only.

Sign up to the mailing list to download the
free Epilogues to Hotwife Sharing Fantasy,
The Hotwife Adventure and Hotwife Training and to be
updated on all future releases.

http://eepurl.com/c3ICWf

prologue
THE
hotwife
ADVENTURE
KARLY VIOLET
ARLY VIOLET
hotwife
TRAINING
EPILOGUE

KARLY VIOLET
EPILOGUE
HOTWIFE
SHARING FANTASY

Before you start reading Watching My Wife

you might also enjoy

Hotwife's Unforgettable Night

[1]

Click to BUY NOW[2]

1. https://books2read.com/u/b6kg1y

2. https://books2read.com/u/b6kg1y

Sign up to my Patreon account and receive exclusive Hotwife stories every month and sexy scenes every week!

https://www.patreon.com/karlyviolet

CONTENTS PAGE

Chapter One: A Shameless Plug
Chapter Two: Dinner Alone
Chapter Three: No Time for Hubby
Chapter Four: Another Piece to the Puzzle
Chapter Five: Hardly Acquaintances
Chapter Six: Ready, Willing, Able
Chapter Seven: A Strapping Young Lad
Chapter Eight: A Profitable Endeavor
Chapter Nine: An Intense Encounter
Chapter Ten: A Proper Business

Chapter One: A Shameless Plug

Shane is completely into the schtick he has memorized for the energy drink mix that he has been using and selling for the last few months. "This is a miracle for a lot of people," he tells me as he pushes three sample packets toward me on the desk. "I've lost thirty pounds over the last two months, Rob. I haven't changed how I eat at all."

I nod my head. "You are looking pretty good," I admit. "So, how many of these do you drink each day?"

He sits up in his seat and smiles. "I have one for breakfast and then one for lunch. Dinner is a healthy, balanced meal."

"Let me get this straight," I reply with a smirk on my face. "You only drink this stuff for breakfast and for lunch and then you eat a meal that is healthy. No burgers or fries?"

"Of course not," he says before adding, "You could allow that once a week maybe as a treat for being good."

I can't help but laugh a little. "You do realize that you are essentially starving yourself for most of the day before eating the sort of meal that you should be eating more than once per day, right? You *have* actually changed the way you eat, Shane." My common sense thoughts on the powdered drink mixes Shane is trying to sell me does not seem to impress my colleague.

"The powder helps to curb your appetite while giving you vital nutrients, Rob. It's good for you."

"Okay." I look down at the pamphlet on the desk in front of me as well as the packets of mix.

"You want to have your own business, right? This is a good way to get started with that, Rob."

I look back up at him. "My own business? Shane, I want to have my own *internet* business, not some sort of multilevel marketing sham."

"I am making over two hundred dollars per month just on social media, man. If I work it a little harder I might be able to double that soon."

I laugh. "I'm afraid that won't support my wife and me. I need something that can generate at least as much as I make here as human resources manager." For the last several months I have lamented the fact that I can't afford to start a side business. The company has been putting out memos to the employees that times are tough and that we should be ready and willing to sacrifice to help keep the place afloat. What is unpleasantly strange, though, is that I have yet to see anyone in upper management sacrifice anything at all. As a matter of fact, they seem to be indulging more and more in trips to international destinations to have their so-called conferences. Perhaps if they took their own warnings seriously they would give the rest of us something to work toward.

"It's a start," Shane replies before changing the subject. "How is Dana's hair salon doing nowadays?"

I sigh. "That national brand is still taking a huge bite out of her clientele base. They undercut her prices and offer a lot that she just can't afford to offer. It's not fair, but it's the way things work sometimes. If I could get something else going we could both move away from our primary jobs and toward more financial independence. As it is, Dana and I are both stuck where we are at."

"But she is trying for that additional training to open a full spa, right?"

"She is, but it has been slow going for the last two months. Dana still doesn't have the bank financing to expand her shop into a day spa." My wife believes that if she upgrades her facility to a day spa she might be able to attract more clients. However, this requires some training by the state as well as money to purchase the additional equipment. None of this has been cheap and it has cost us most of our savings so far.

"It will work out," Shane reassures me. "In the meantime, you should consider selling this product." He taps one of the packs of mix with his fingers. "You know a lot of people, man. I'm sure that if you could get just three of your friends to sign up as distributors you would be very happy with the income that you would begin to receive."

Chuckling, I shake my head. "I don't like trying to get other people to sell stuff for me, Shane. Doesn't it bother you just a little to try to get me or someone else you know to sell these drink mixes?"

He smiles. "You have to think of this product as something that other people will be helped by, Rob. If you give the samples a try I think that you will see just how effective the product can be."

I smile. "You have gotten pretty good at this, haven't you?"

Shane nods his head. "It's what I do now, bro." We both laugh before the conversation becomes a bit more serious. "They are going to let me go soon, Rob."

Shaking my head, I reply, "What do you mean they are going to let you go?"

"The company. Look, you and I both know that they don't need me here. The writing has been on the wall for the last year or so. I'm a sixth toe on an already ugly foot. Pretty soon upper management will see this and they will have me tossed out. This thing I am doing with the drink mixes is just a way to prepare for that."

"For one thing, they are not going to fire you, Shane. For another, that side gig you have going with those supplements will never make you enough money to live off of."

"It could," he argues. "If I get enough people to distribute it beneath me."

"Multilevel marketing," I say for the second time in the last few minutes. "It rarely works for guys like us. Shane, if you are really so worried about losing your job here you should get a resume together and start looking around just in case."

He nods his head as he tells me, "I have already done that. The thing is, the other places nearby that might be willing to hire a human resources manager don't need one. I'm a lost cause, Rob." Shane's dark brown eyes seem sad and distant as he shakes his head. Maybe this is what has propelled him to get into better shape over the last few months? He knows that at least a third of what it takes to get you hired is your presentation during an interview. The man is already partially bald, so getting his body into better shape is all he can do to get that first impression right.

"I don't think they will fire you," I say again. "You're a great guy, Shane. When there are problems that arise with employees you are great at what you do to help out."

"You are here too. Rob, they only need *one* human resources manager and I'm just not as good at this job as you are."

I shrug my shoulders. "I think you are wrong on that one, buddy. If I get my own business off the ground I will probably get the hell out of here myself. They are going to need you when I do that."

"I'll lose my job before you get that online thing off the ground," my colleague muses. The idea that I will somehow get some sort of business going anytime soon has been a running joke inside our small human resources office. Shane and I know each other very well. We understand the difficulties we each face and how badly we want to be free from the dictates of the assholes upstairs. Even so, we are both attached to the company structure very much like a couple of kittens latched onto their mother cat's nipples. If we let go of them too soon go we are going to starve to death.

"They won't fire you," I tell him for a third time. "Just hang in there, alright? Everything will be better soon. Just wait and see." Shane smiles as he gets up from his chair and stands there for a moment.

"Hey, I'm going to go get a cup of coffee in the lobby. Can I get you anything while I am there, Rob?"

"Sure. I'll take a cup of coffee with sugar and creamer, please."

"No problem." Shane turns and walks out of the human resources office and I find myself alone with my thoughts.

"You fucking pricks," I say as I look up at the ceiling above me. For the last couple of years the upper management at this company, including the company's CEO, has done nothing but sow discontent and worry within the rank and file employees of the company. Every month or so an email memo is circulated that warns of impending doom if things do not turn around for the company. It is as if the management upstairs thinks that the average employee here can miraculously do something to stem whatever rising economic tide is sure to wash us away. Why do they tell us that things are bad when there is practically nothing we peons can do to stop the supposed crisis?

"Hey, do you have a minute?" One of the company's newer employees, Lisa Salvador, walks into the office and I turn my chair toward her before standing up.

"Good morning. What can I do for you?" I struggle to put a smile on my face as I walk up to her. I hired Lisa to work in the accounting department about six months ago. Though a bit of a nervous nelly, she has the acumen of a sharp financial auditor.

"It's about Jeremy," she replies. "I can't take it anymore."

I shake my head. "What has he done now?"

Lisa sighs. "I hate to complain, but he went through my desk drawers again this morning. I think he is a kleptomaniac, Rob." Her blue eyes are piercing as she looks into mine. An attractive woman in her early twenties, I have had more than a few naughty thoughts about her.

"Again?" I have warned Jeremy not to touch other people's things, but he seems almost driven to continue to do so. "Did he take anything this time?"

"Well, no, not that I could tell. I still don't want him going through my desk drawers."

"Did you see him do it?"

Lisa shakes her head. "I didn't see him do it this time, but I did notice that things were out of order on my desk after I came back from the copier room. Janice and Brian both saw him go through my drawers, though."

"Did you ask him why he did it?"

"I asked him what he was doing and he claimed that he was looking for some chewing gum." After a brief pause, Lisa continues, "He knows that I don't chew gum, Rob. He's a *snooper* and I am tired of it."

Nodding my head, I tell her, "I'll have another talk with him."

"Please do more than just talk to him this time, Rob," Lisa pleads with me. "Jeremy gives me the creeps. No one should have to work around someone like him." The young woman turns and after giving me one last look leaves and closes the office door behind her.

"Fuck." I shake my head as I think of the problematic employee. I have a difficult decision to make and I really do not want to make it. "You stupid jackass," I say of Jeremy as I walk over to my desk and sit back down. I have no choice; he has to go. After three separate warnings to stay out of other people's things, he has finally pushed the line too far. Whatever issues he has that drive him to look through desks and purses, I know he is not a thief. Still, Jeremy will have to work this out somewhere else. We cannot afford to lose someone as talented as Lisa just because I do not want to fill another empty spot in their office. "You've signed your own pink slip," I say quietly as I begin typing on my computer. By the end of the day, Jeremy will have his final paycheck and I will be looking for another employee to take his place. It is a difficult and sad thing to do, but he has to go.

Chapter Two: Dinner Alone

I miss Dana when she goes to her training for the new spa she is going to open. SHe needs to be able to compete with a franchise of the national hair salon that moved in a short distance from her own shop several months ago, so I have decided to support her in this goal and keep my thoughts about it to myself. Though my wife has not wanted in the past to open anything like a full-service spa, she has finally given in and began the training for the state licensure to do so. It is her hope, as well as mine, that this will help to turn around her business before it is too late.

"Hello, my old friend," I say as I pull a microwave dinner from the freezer. Opening the box, I think of how simple it is to have a meal when Dana is not around. Though I don't mind having a frozen meal for any dinner, my wife is far from satisfied with such things when she is around. We often rotate our cooking responsibilities from one evening to the next, but since I am left alone I will heat up a cold meatloaf and mashed potatoes meal to enjoy while I am surfing the internet on the computer in the spare bedroom. If things go well, I will probably find myself watching some Netflix videos as well before dropping into bed and getting some sleep.

My cell phone suddenly vibrates and I pick it up from the kitchen countertop as the meal is cooking inside the microwave. "How are you doing, babe?" I smile as I read the message from Dana.

I text her back. "I'm great, sexy. How are you enjoying your training?"

A frowning emoji is sent back almost immediately with a message. "I hate these things, Rob. You know that."

"I'm sorry." I smile to myself as I think about all the times that my wife has complained about having to go back to get more training just to keep her shop open. Though it is necessary in order to compete with the national competitor nearby, Dana is not a fan of putting tanning beds and a massage room in her place of business.

"What are you making for dinner?" she asks.

Chuckling, I respond, "Meatloaf. Yummy." I add a smiling emoji to the end of the text message and send it to her. She soon replies with an emoji that represents someone vomiting. How Dana finds these emojis on her phone is a mystery to me. All I know to use are the ones that are readily available on the small task bar just above my texting keyboard.

"I had spaghetti for lunch and dinner will be served by the training center later. I hear it will be chicken marsala."

"Oh? They must have stock in an Italian eatery somewhere." I laugh as I send the message and Dana soon answers back.

"They probably do. I have to go now, Rob. I just wanted to wish you a good night and a nice sleep? Oh, and don't invite any other women over for naked Twister tonight, alright?" This has been an inside joke between us for the entire time we have been married. Dana one time told me that the only way I could invite any women over when she was not home was if I was going to play naked twister with them. It was meant as tongue in cheek, but of course, we have kept it going since then.

"You behave too." I send a heart emoji to her and say, "I love you."

"I love you too, sweetheart. See you tomorrow night." This ends our texting and it is just in time as I reach into the microwave and remove the now-hot meal. Placing it onto a fabric pad, I carry the meal and a glass of water to the spare bedroom. After putting everything down on the small desk, I sit down and turn on the computer.

Relaxing in the chair as I take a sip of the cool water in the glass, I move the mouse around on the top of the desk and open up my Facebook account. Though I am not the most dedicated to looking at social media sites, I sometimes use it to just unwind from the day and to see how other people I know are doing. As I do, I see a message that was sent to me from someone else. Though I normally do not open messages from unknown people, I go ahead and do so now and read the message.

"You know me," the message begins as I sit forward in my seat. "Though, I won't tell you who I am right now." Shaking my head, I scroll down through the small message box and see a link toward the bottom with the words, "You should know what is happening. Don't hate the messenger."

"What the fuck?" I say to myself as I raise an eyebrow. Just now, all the warnings I have gotten from the IT department at work concerning not opening links from unknown senders floods back to my mind. "Who the hell are you?" I say to myself as I click on the name in the message box. This person, calling themselves *Orange Panda,* has a Facebook page with no previous history before today. My concern spikes as I shake my head. Suddenly, another message comes through from the same unknown source.

"Are you there?"

I could block this individual. Maybe I should, but I don't. Instead, I ask, "Who are you?"

A response comes back seconds later. "Rob, I'm a friend of Dana's and I have been over to your house before. You know me."

Shaking my head, I reply, "Then tell me who you are."

"I can't." After a short pause, another message to me says, "I swear, that link is legit. You can trust me, Rob. You need to see what is there."

Frowning, I ask again, "Who are you?"

"Please, Rob," the person replies. "Just look at it. I can't tell you who I am right now." The message then ends with, "You will thank me later. Watch the video." The green light next to the name Orange Panda in the message box suddenly turns off. Whoever this person is, they have logged out of Messenger for now and I am left with a choice to make.

"Fuck." I wring my hands together as I think about the strange message that was sent to me. "Do I click it and get a virus on my computer or not?" I muse as I look at the blue link in the earlier message. "How did they know my name?" I ask as I run my finger over the mouse button. If I click on the link it could open something that ruins my computer immediately. It could also share some secret with me that I will be happy to know. At least, this is according to Orange Panda, whoever the hell that happens to be.

"Just do it," I tell my hand as I clench my teeth together. Clicking the link, I wait for some crazy box to pop up that will tell me my computer is locked and that they now want a million dollars to unlock my computer and retrieve my files. Instead, a small box with a video comes up. The video begins to play as two people in a dark room are having sex.

"You are so tight, baby," the man says in the dark as his hips thrust hard toward the woman in the bed. "Fucking whore. *Bitch.* You are so *hot.*" He slaps the side of her ass hard as he pushes her legs back and begins to move faster. "Fucking whore. I want to come inside of you."

"Come inside me," the woman squeals as her petite little body moves violently beneath him.

"Dammit, you are so sexy." He reaches down and twists the woman's nipples hard as he pulls on them.

"OWWWW!" I cringe as I watch the hard sex between the two people taking place.

"Get up," he commands as he pulls his long cock out of her wet pussy. The woman immediately complies and I am able to see her blue eyes briefly. She soon has turned around and gotten on all fours as the man pushes into her asshole.

"Shit!" The voice is almost familiar as the woman groans. *"Fuck!"*

"You wanted this, right?" the man asks his lover. "You wanted me to show you a fun time, didn't you?" He slaps her ass hard and she flinches as his balls slap her labia. He then reaches forward and grabs her long hair, placed into a ponytail, and pulls it hard as he fucks her.

"Ohhhh..."

"Quiet, *bitch,*" he tells her as he slaps her ass hard again. I flinch as I see the handprint appearing on her ass cheek.

"What the fuck is this?" I say with a nervous chuckle as I continue to watch the video. Though I am not certain who either person is in the video, it appears to be something that one of my friends has sent me as a joke. "Shane?" I shake my head as I quickly move that thought from my mind. Though my colleague at work enjoys the occasional practical joke, he would have never sent me something like this. My mind begins to bring up the names and faces of all the other people I know both professionally and personally. There are maybe four or five who are capable of pulling off a joke like this, but only one or two who would really want to.

"Why this video?" I ask as I shake my head. "What am I supposed to see here?" Whatever it is, I get hard regardless. The two people in the video are in a dark room and fucking each other hard and fast. I watch as they both come, the man blowing his jism into the woman's ass before he pulls out of her and then turns around to turn off the camera. With the video at an end, I remain confused as to what this has to do with me.

"Leo?" I say as I shake my head again. I have not seen Leo Richards in more than three years. We used to hang out together a lot when we were younger, but our worlds are now miles apart, both physically and otherwise, since he moved to California to work for an electronics company. He used to send me sexually explicit videos as a lark at one time, but I have not heard from him for a long time now. It cannot be him, can it?

Goosebumps rise along my neck as I restart the video and watch it again. I begin to eat my meal as it is getting cold. Once again, I watch as the man takes the woman in the video forcefully, her body quivering with every thrust of his long, hard manhood. I pre-come a little into my pants and wonder if I know the guy. There are lots of men who I work with who might film themselves while having sex, but I can't think of specifically who this guy could be. It would help if I could see his face better, but that is likely an impossibility. I am lucky to see as much as I do with the terrible lighting in the room they are in.

"This is shit," I finally say as I close the video and the message box. "Pure shit." I sigh as I think about what other reasons I might have been asked by the stranger to open the video and watch it. There could have been a virus embedded inside it, so I begin a scan with the antivirus program on my computer. "I'll catch you if you are a little fucker looking for my information," I say as I sit back and watch the process. After taking another bite of my cold food, I make a quick decision. "I'm going out." Tired of the microwave meal, I get up from my chair and go to the living room to put on my shoes. I want more than just reheated meatloaf. I want a steak now that I have had my sexual appetite whetted by the video I have watched. Maybe if I fill my stomach I can forget what I have seen this evening. It seems like someone has wasted my time with the porn video in my message box. Though I appreciate watching a good fucking video like any other man, the film was poorly made and dark. It is not worth any more of my attention tonight.

Chapter Three: No Time for Hubby

"Oh, hello!" Dana's eyes are wide as she is surprised to see me standing on the other side of the threshold to let her into our house.

"Let me take that," I say as I reach for her rolling suitcase. As I do, I tell her, "I took the afternoon off from work to see you come home, honey."

"How sweet." She smiles at me and hands over the handle of the suitcase. Dana comes inside and closes the door behind her as I move her suitcase to the bedroom. I come back quickly and take her into my arms to kiss her.

"I missed you," I say to my wife as I smile at her. "How was everything?"

Dana's blue eyes meet mine as she holds me close. "It was fine. The flight was a little boring, but all in all, it was a good trip." We release each other and walk over to the sofa where we have a seat next to each other. "How were things here?"

I nod my head. "Everything was fine. It's nice to see you back here, though. I don't like sitting around the house at night without you."

"That's so sweet of you." Dana kisses me again before saying, "I can't wait to take a shower and just chill out."

"Me too." As I watch my wife get up from the sofa, I ask, "What about some Chinese food? Or Italian? I could order something and have it here pretty quickly, honey."

Dana sighs. "I don't want anything to eat right now." Her eyes seem to hold some kind of unknown truth that I have yet to discover.

"Is everything alright?" I ask.

She nods her head. "All I want to do is take a shower and lie down in bed if that's okay, Rob." My wife turns and walks toward the bedroom as my stomach growls. For a moment, I consider calling for an order of food anyway, but I do not want to seem as if I am being inconsiderate of Dana's feelings. So, I get up and follow her into the bedroom.

"I'm sorry that you don't feel well," I tell her as we go through the door. "Can I get the shower ready for you?"

Dana shakes her head. "I really could use some time to myself, Rob."

"To yourself?" My heart sinks as I realize my wife is asking me to leave her entirely alone. "What happened, honey? You know you can talk to me, right?"

She turns her blue eyes toward me and shakes her head. "Can't you just leave me alone for now? What do I have to do to get that through to you, Rob?"

"What?" A chill runs down my neck and back as I feel my face turn red. "Have I done something to upset you?"

"Just leave, Rob." The command is cold and harsh as I continue to look into Dana's eyes. Something is wrong and I want to be supportive of my wife, but I also feel as if she is being a little too rude in trying to make space for herself away from me.

"Alright, I will," I reply as I turn quickly and march out of the room. "I can't believe this." I make the mistake of saying the second part a bit too loudly as Dana hears it and follows me to the living room.

"You don't understand what it's like to sit through three long days of training for that shit, Rob. If you did, you wouldn't complain."

"Complain about what?" I ask as I spin back around.

"You do this any time I ask you for just a little time to myself. We can always order out tomorrow, Rob. Today has been a really tough day for me."

"That's fine," I reply as I continue to try to keep my composure. "But sometimes I feel like you are just pushing me away, Dana. Why do you want to push me away?"

"I'm not fucking pushing you away!" My wife raises her voice before going to the sofa and sitting down. "Now you have my attention, Rob. Like a petulant little child you have asked for it, so here you are. Tell me about your fucking day."

Shaking my head, I sit down in a chair nearby. I do not know at first what to make of this sudden outpouring of anger from my wife, but I do know that I need to try to keep things as calm as I possibly can.

Something has happened and I do not want to cause Dana any further anger by prodding her.

"I'm sorry that you are upset. All I wanted was to have a quiet meal with you and watch some television, honey. We can do that on another night when you feel better." I mistakenly think that this is the end of the strife. It is not.

"And sex, right? You want to wine me and dine me and fuck me tonight, don't you? Isn't that where this is all going, Rob? Your mind is always on sex."

"What?" I say incredulously. "Dana, I didn't say anything about sex. We don't have to get anything to eat or watch a movie. It's fine. We can talk about this tomorrow."

Dana sits forward on the sofa. "You are so selfish sometimes."

"Stop it. Please." I shake my head as I look over at her. "I just said that I'm not pushing for anything, honey. Please, let's just drop it. Go take a shower and then hop into bed. I love you. Don't be so upset with me."

Though at first it appears that my wife will leave and do as she has told me she wants to do, Dana stands to her feet and continues with her rant. "I knew the moment that I stepped through the door that you were going to start an argument with me."

Finally done with trying to take the higher ground, I retort, "*You* started this argument, my love. I have tried to back out of it so that you can relax like you told me that you wanted to. *You* are the one who can't let this go."

"Fuck you." The reply is cold and hard as her blue eyes stare into me. Dana has the capacity to be callous and crude when she wants to be, and apparently she has decided that I deserve a large measure of that wrath this afternoon.

"Holy shit." I stand to my feet and walk toward the kitchen. "I love you, Dana. I'm finished with this back and forth, though." In the kitchen, I reach for a glass in a cabinet and then get some water from the faucet.

As I take a drink I hear my wife walk in and begin once again to chide me for whatever wrong I have committed upon her.

"How is that online business thing coming together, *Rob?* Have you spent any time with that, *Rob?* Do you plan to actually do anything with your life other than complain, *ROB?*" Dana knows how sensitive I am about my lack of advancement in the business I have been trying to start. It is the source of some tension between us at times because of the two thousand dollars I borrowed from our savings account to get the website ready.

"Dana, leave it alone," I warn her as I put the glass of water down on the countertop.

"Leave it alone? Just like you left me alone when I got home?"

I turn to face her. "What the hell are you doing?" Glaring at Dana, I clench my jaw as I shake my head. "You are trying to cause me pain. Why are you doing this? I don't deserve it."

"You deserve this and more," Dana retorts as she pokes me in the chest with her finger. "You are a *fuck-up,* Rob. Because you are a *fuck-up,* I am trying to help my business so that we don't suffer any more than we have to financially. As a *fuck-up,* you don't have the right to question me or what I do."

"I'm not a fuck-up!" I growl back. "And I didn't say anything about what you are doing. Dammit, Dana...what the hell are you doing?" I walk away from her again and Dana continues to follow me. My mind is racing as I try to understand what it is that is motivating my wife to be so vindictive and angry. What have I done to cause her to be this way with me? I have not seen her in three days and now she behaves as if I have done something to her recently.

"You don't like hearing the truth, do you?"

"I'm done," I say as I walk toward the spare bedroom.

"Of course you are. Be that way, Rob."

"Goodnight, honey." I smile at her briefly as I try to bring my own anger to heel. Dana gives me one last frown before turning and walking to our bedroom. She slams the door and I hear the lock turn in the doorknob. Tonight I will be sleeping in the spare bedroom instead of beside my wife.

After closing the door, I ask myself, "What the fuck did I do?" I sit down in the small chair in front of the desk where the computer is already turned on. As I move the mouse along and look at a news website, I try to forget the exchange between the two of us. "I didn't do anything, though," I answer myself as my mind continues to examine everything I have said to Dana the last few days by text or email. Everything seemed so sweet and innocent to me when she got home. Did she take anything the wrong way? All I offered was dinner earlier and that set her off. Why did it set her off?

Looking down at a small message box that appears on the computer screen, I open it and see that Orange Panda is back. "Did you watch the video?" the person asks me.

At first, I do not want to respond. Even though my antivirus program did not detect an infection in the earlier video, it does not mean there is not one to be had by viewing links in messages. "I looked at it," I tell the unknown person. "I don't get why you sent me a porn video, though."

"A porn video? That's all you think that it is? Man, you are so clueless."

"Clueless?" It seems that yet another person has decided to poke at me this afternoon and I am not in the mood to put up with it. "Fuck you."

"Fuck me?" I'm sure the response is surprising to Orange Panda as I scowl at the screen. "Why do I even try to help you?"

"Help me? How are you helping me? Who the hell are you? Tell me that and then I will decide if you are actually trying to help me."

"Dude, no." I think for a moment as I try to recall which of Dana's friends or our mutual acquaintances would call me *dude*. None come to mind at the moment, which does not surprise me.

"You are a scammer, aren't you?" I prod. "One of those who look for something after you hook your victims. I am not the guy you want to fuck with, DUDE."

"Shit, Rob." This is quickly followed by, "I will get you a better video. Be ready." This is the last of the messages from the unknown person before the green dot next to their name dims.

"All I need now is some fucking wacko talking to me on a messenger," I lament as I sit back in my chair. "My wife is off her keel and now this jackass come back to bother me." Taking a long, deep breath," I relax in my chair as I look at the walls of the spare bedroom. I have no idea what is happening in my life right now. That seems par for the course with me, though. After all, I am a major *fuck-up* who has made Dana's life a living hell. If only I could understand how to not do that things would be so much better for the both of us.

Chapter Four: Another Piece to the Puzzle

I wake up the next morning and roll out of the small bed in the spare bedroom. Walking to the door of the bedroom, I open it and see that the master bedroom door is open. I make my way over to see if Dana is up yet and she is. However, she is not in the bedroom nor does she appear to be in the house at all. My wife likely got up early and went to her hair salon to start the day now that she is back in town. I turn and walk over to the computer.

"Forgot to turn it off," I say to myself as I move the mouse and look at the screen as it comes to life. There is a message box on the screen that must have popped up sometime late last night from Orange Panda, so I sit down in the chair at the desk and open it to read.

"Here you are," the stranger says unceremoniously with a link to another video. "This should clear some things up."

"Okay," I mutter as I click on the link without much thought this time. Making myself comfortable in the chair, I wait as the video window opens up and soon begins to play.

"Oh, fuck, Raul," the woman says as she squeaks. She is riding the man and he is focusing on her breasts as he films the encounter with her.

"They're real, right?" he asks.

"As real as they get." The camera pans up to the woman's face and my heart skips a beat or two as I realize who it is.

"Fuck, Dana," I mutter as I look at her face in the video. "What the hell is this?" Shaking my head, I feel my face turn deep red as I see her riding on the man's hard cock. She seems happy as she moves her pelvis around on him.

"You are so deep, Raul," she tells the man as she bends down and kisses him. Dana then sits back up and asks him, "Do you like the way my pussy feels, Raul?"

"I love it," he replies quickly as he breathes heavily.

"Then tell me that you do," my wife says to him. "Tell me that my pussy feels good on your dick, Raul."

The man behind the camera chuckles. "I love the way your soft pussy feels on my dick, Dana. It's so tight. It's so wet." My own cock becomes hard as I hear the stranger say that to her.

"Are you going to come inside me?"

"Fuck, you don't want me to pull out? I could get you pregnant."

"I don't care," she tells the man as she grinds hard into him.

"Damn, not so hard," he pleads with Dana as she reaches down and pinches his nipples. "You are a wild one, aren't you?"

"I can be." My wife bends down and begins to nibble at the man's nipples as she continues to move her pelvis around with his stiff cock inside her muff. I pre-come a little as I think about how lucky he is.

"Oh, you slick little minx," he groans as Dana sits up and begins to move faster and faster on his hard shaft. Raul reaches up and cups one of her round breasts, fondling it carefully as he enjoys the way my wife is fucking him. "Shit, I'm going to come soon, Dana. Are you sure that you don't want me to wear a rubber?"

"I'm coming already," she squeaks. Dana leans back on him and now her swollen clitoris is easy to see as the man zooms the camera in on where his cock is moving in and out of her pussy. "Fuck, Raul...*UHHHH!!!*" My wife begins to come as she slides up and down the man's pole. *"Ohhhh...NAHHHH!!!"* Her petite body quivers as she enjoys his manhood buried deep inside her sweet twat.

"You are so fucking...*FUCK!!!*" The camera shakes as Raul begins to come inside my wife. *"Ahhhh...ohhhh...nahhhh...uhhhh..."* As he comes inside her, his white man sauce oozes out of her hole as Dana moves quickly up and down his cock. *"Ohhhh!!!"*

"RAUL!!! FUCK!!!" My wife's naked body quakes as she squirts a little, spraying her lover's crotch with her sweet nectar as she finishes having an orgasm. She seems happy as she finishes up with him and then lifts her tight pussy away from his still-swollen stalk.

Raul points the camera at my wife as he asks her, "Are you alright, sweetie?"

"Oh, fuck, I'm good," Dana giggles as she looks over at the man and smiles. "I wish we had done a little more before we came, though."

He laughs. "We have all night, right? Let's take our time and have some fun, Dana. The night is ours." The man then moves the camera so that my wife's face is alongside his. I do not recognize the man who has just filled Dana's pecan pie with his special icing, but I do know that he is called Raul in the video.

"What the fuck?" I say quietly as I sit back in my chair after the video ends. Though it appears to be just a snippet of a larger video, it is enough for me to know exactly what Orange Panda tried to tell me with the first video. The last one was of poor quality, which is why I could not see the point of it to begin with.

I sit up in my chair and type a message to the person who sent the video to me. "Are you there?" The green light is on, but that does not necessarily mean that anyone will receive the message on the other end right now.

After a minute or two, a reply comes back. "I'm here."

Sighing, I type into the message box, "I saw the video. Was it the same two people as in the first video."

"Just her. The guys are different."

"Oh." I don't know what else to say as I sit quietly and stare at the computer screen. I should feel as if I have been cheated upon by my wife, but Dana and I have had our sexual adventures before. I suppose I am just irritated that she decided to go on an adventure of her own without asking or telling me about it.

"She has been with several other men," the person on the other end of the conversation tells me. "Dana is cheating on you, Rob."

I swallow hard as I reply, "Who are you? Surely you don't think that I will tell Dana who gave me the videos."

"I can't do that," Orange Panda replies. "There are just too many bridges that could be burned down if I tell you. Besides, it really doesn't matter who I am. What matters is that you need to know what is going on. Dana is being unfaithful."

I grimace as I think of who the person could be. It really doesn't matter, I suppose, but curiosity is a difficult thing to control when you want so badly to know things. I am an extremely curious guy by nature anyway. "What else do you know?" I ask.

"Nothing much," the person answers. "Just what you saw in the video. There are other videos, but it has been difficult to get the first two. I'm not sure that I could get any more, but I think there could be at least three of four more of them that may be available."

I shake my head. "How many men have there been?"

My heart thumps inside my chest hard as I wait for a response. I do not have to wait long before there is a reply. "I'm not sure. Maybe ten."

"Ten?" I say out loud without typing it into the message box. "Fuck, Dana. What the hell have you been up to? And you had the audacity to argue with *me* last night? Really?" Again, it is not the thought that my wife is fucking other men that bothers me so much. It is that she treated me so poorly last night when I really did not deserve it. Dana is having sex without me and I should have known about this before it happened. There is much that I need to say to her when I see her next.

"I'm sorry if this shocks you," Orange Panda says to me. "The ball is now in your court."

I nod my head and reply in the message box. "Thank you for sending these videos to me. I'll have to look into it what my wife is up to."

"No problem, buddy. I'll see you around." The green light beside the Orange Panda names suddenly goes dim again and our conversation ends.

"Okay," I say as I take a quick breath. "What do I do now?" The first video is practically worthless to me, but the one I watched moments ago is very clear. There is no doubt who stars in the video and I know that Dana will have no way to claim that there is some mistake. No, she will have to answer my questions about this no matter what she might think about me asking her about it.

"You are being selfish," I mock my wife as I think about the same line she used on me just last night. "All you care about is yourself." I begin to steam as I think about how she reacted angrily to me last night. I did not deserve the anger Dana exploded with and directed at me after she got home from her training. All I did was try to make her feel welcome by offering her dinner and a quiet evening with me. "Sex," I laugh. "She accused me of trying to get sex from her. Well, fuck. What did these guys do that was so much better than what I tried?" I laugh quietly as I sit back in my chair and think about Dana's time away from home. There is no doubt that she has used some of her time away from here to meet other men for these little trysts. I am amazed that she was okay with them filming her, though. That is the sort of thing my wife has resisted doing with me in the past.

"How shitty of you," I say quietly as I shake my head. "You really treated me badly." I need to get over this. I cannot allow my irritation for the way things happened last night to continue to control how I feel about my wife. It is important that I keep my emotions in check when I ask Dana about these men later.

"This afternoon," I tell myself as I get up and walk into the master bedroom. "When she gets home you will have to have a conversation. This has to be cleared up as soon as possible." Today would be a good day to spend the morning, a Saturday morning, out at the park to clear my head before I speak to Dana. So, I get dressed and leave the house to do just that.

Chapter Five: Hardly Acquaintances

"Hello, Rob." The attitude that Dana exudes as she walks into our house is completely different than what I encountered just twenty-four hours earlier.

"Hey, honey," I say coolly as she walks into the spare bedroom. I am sitting in front of the computer after having a long walk in the city park today before going to get some lunch at one of my favorite restaurants.

"What have you been up to?" Dana sits down on the bed nearby as she smiles at me.

I smile back. "Well, I went for a walk and then came back here to surf online a little. Not much to do today, really."

"That's nice." My wife's eyes move from me to the computer and then back to me again. "So, about last night," Dana begins as she looks away from me for a moment. "I think we both got a little carried away."

I can't help but allow a quick chuckle as she says this. "Well, okay. Maybe we got a little too heated."

Dana's eyes look hard at me as she attempts to understand why I would laugh about this. "Yeah, we were both in the wrong."

"Okay. Where was *I* wrong?" I should not push like this, I know, but I hate letting her make me feel as if I am the one who caused the argument we had last night. If anything, I was the one trying to put out the fire as it began to roar to life.

My wife sighs. "I really don't want to rehash anything, do you?" She smiles uneasily as she tries to move past what happened yesterday.

Nodding my head, I reply, "Alright. Then I have a question for you, Dana."

"Sure." She smiles again as she nods her head.

"What is going on behind my back that you happen to be involved in?"

"What?"

"What is happening with you that I don't know about. I'm just curious, my love. What are you doing that I should know about?" I watch my wife's body language as she moves around where she is seated on the bed.

"Nothing," she answers. "I have been working on the shop and going to training sessions. That's all." Dana fidgets slightly as she looks nervously at me. There is something there that she does not want me to see.

"Well, I was given a little video by a friend of yours in my messenger. Would you like to see it?"

My wife slowly nods her head. "Alright. What is it?" She gets up from the bed and walks over to stand beside me at the desk. I open the window of the second video clip that I had minimized and click on it. The look on Dana's face is immediate and surprised as she sees the naked bodies in the video. "I don't know the name of the sender," I tell Dana as she watches her naked body moving up and down the other man's cock. "But they call themself *Orange Panda*. It's a weird name, which is why I almost didn't watch the videos in the first place."

"Videos?" Dana says quietly as she puts a hand over her mouth.

"I received two videos." I sit quietly as I watch the images on the screen. My wife is speechless for a time as she watches herself pleasuring another man. I say nothing as I realize how well the video itself delivers a message already. When it finally ends, Dana goes back to the bed and sits down.

After a couple of minutes of silence, she tells me, "I'm sorry, Rob."

Nodding my head, I reply, "For what? The thing you are doing in this video? Or for the way that you treated me yesterday afternoon, Dana?"

My wife turns her blue eyes toward me. "You know that I don't love him, right? It was just sex."

"Sure, it was just sex," I reply. "But you didn't tell me that you were thinking about having sex with another man, did you? We have had an agreement for a while that if either of us thought about doing something with another person we would talk to each other about it first. You didn't do that."

"No, I didn't," she admits softly.

"And then you come home and tear into me as if I have done something horrible to you. What am I supposed to think after seeing these videos and getting berated by you the way that I was, Dana?"

My wife shakes her head. "I'm sorry."

Though I want to say something hurtful to her, I do not. She is my wife, after all, and I love her completely. "Okay, then. How many guys have you been with behind my back?"

Dana looks up to me and shakes her head. "Don't ask me that, Rob."

"Why not? Are there more?"

She swallows hard as she looks into my eyes. "Please. I don't want to tell you that. I'm so embarrassed that I have allowed it to go this far."

"*This* far?"

"Rob, you have to understand why I did not tell you about them in the first place. I figured that you might think that I have gone too far with my desires. Please, let's just focus on getting past this."

"I need to know," I reply flatly.

My wife looks into my eyes for a while before looking away and admitting to me, "There have been around ten."

"Ten?" I almost laugh as I speak the number. Apparently Orange Panda's count is right on the money. "Holy hell, Dana. Where are you finding these guys?"

She shrugs her shoulders. "I met most of them online. They were willing to meet up with me and have sex."

"And come inside you," I comment. "I can't believe you have hidden ten guys from me like this. Fuck, you are a busy woman."

"Please, Rob," Dana says to me with tears in her eyes. "They mean nothing to me."

I shake my head. "You know that is not entirely true, right? They mean *something* to you. It might not be love, but it is definitely something. You wanted to get off with other men without me knowing about it, didn't you?"

Her face red, my wife replies, "Yes. Rob, you have to understand why I have done this. I wanted to experience these men without you expecting to have a threesome with us."

"So, instead of *me* being selfish as you claimed yesterday, *you* have been selfish?" Of course I want to push this line with Dana. She was mean and rude to me after I offered to be nothing but sweet to her. I did not deserve what she said to me and I suppose I am still a little hurt by it.

"Yeah. I'm the selfish one," my wife replies quietly. "I'm sorry, Rob." She gets up from the bed and walks over to me. Reaching over, Dana takes my hand into hers and then pulls close to me. "How can I make this up to you?"

Smiling softly, I reply, "You know that I love you, honey. I want you to be happy and I want to be a part of whatever you do. That includes the sex that you have been having with these other men. We promised to let each other know about these things, right? I'm here for you and you are here for me."

"You're right."

"So, here is what I want to do," I tell her. "I want you to keep having sex like this, but I want to film it when it happens."

"What?" Dana's eyes widen.

"Look, you obviously don't have a problem with being filmed, do you? I have two videos of you with other men and I was told by Orange Panda that there are other videos. I want to be the guy who films you and I want to put the videos on my website."

"Rob, your website is set up to sell things."

"And what things am I supposed to sell, Dana?"

She shakes her head. "I don't know. You never quite figured that out."

"Right. Everything is already set up, honey. There is already a way to log in to the website and pay with a credit card and streaming ability is also up and ready to go. All I have to do is add content and advertise."

"But, Rob," she says as she looks at me. "That would mean that my face would be on those videos."

"Yeah, I know," I say as I get hard. "That could be fun, huh?"

"Are you okay with that?"

I nod my head. "I am. Are you?" I smile as I watch Dana's face. She seems worried about the prospect of having videos of her fucking other men distributed from my website. But at the same time, there seems to be a bit of excitement at the thought of doing this with me. Could it be that my wife is willing to do this? Could this be a new business opportunity for both of us?"

"Rob, this is crazy," Dana finally tells me. "Maybe it is crazy enough to work, though."

"Maybe," I reply. "Honey, we have nothing to lose. You like to have sex and I want to film you while you have sex." This also takes care of my desire to get to see her with other men. I am hard even now as I think about watching her having sex while I capture every intimate moment on video.

"Okay, Rob, let's try it," she says softly to me. Her body quivers as I touch her and I smile. "I really am sorry about the way that I behaved with you yesterday too. I think the fact that I was keeping this from you was beginning to wear on me and it finally spilled over when I got home. I was tired and pissed off."

I laugh. "Wow, you were *really* pissed off," I concur. "From now on we need to keep each other in the loop, alright? No more sex behind each other's back, Dana. We have done a good job of letting each other enjoy sex with other people, so let's not allow anything to keep us from doing that in the future? We need to always be honest and open with each other."

"Agreed," my wife says as she smiles at me and gives me a quick kiss. "Would you like to take me out for dinner now?"

Raising one eyebrow, I ask, "Are you going to be a good girl if I take you out?"

Dana laughs and says, "Of course, my love. I'm always a good girl, right?" We both laugh as we kiss again.

"Yeah, right," I answer as she pulls away and walks out of the room to get ready. I sit back in my chair and think about what I have found out over the last few minutes. Dana has been finding plenty of other men to warm their cocks inside of her and that excites me. We will now work together to keep this going as I film each time my wife brings someone to bed.

"Nice," I say as I see Orange Panda's message light turn green. Though I am tempted to message them and say that things are worked out, I do not. As far as I am concerned, there is no longer any reason to speak to the unknown person on the other end of the message box. Whoever it is has accomplished what they said they wanted to accomplish. They told me what was happening with my wife behind my back and I have resolved it with her. Case closed. Now we are going to use what is happening with Dana to make a little extra money while we both enjoy the sexual rush of it. How could this have ended any better?

Chapter Six: Ready, Willing, Able

Dana looks nervously at the computer screen as I scroll from one page to the next. "They are all interested, honey," I tell her with a smile on my face. "Every single one of them have asked to meet you. They *want* you."

My wife shakes her head as she considers the profiles of the men on the computer screen. "How did you do this again?"

Nodding my head and smiling at her, I answer, "I went to three different websites that allows paid advertisements for sex partners. At each website I posted a description of you, including that you are married, and asked for men who would be cool with being filmed having sex with you. I also made it known that they would have to sign away their rights to the video and that their only payment is the sex they get to have with you." My cock stiffens as I hear myself talk about other men fucking Dana. This is something that has always given me a boner, even before we were married to each other.

"You didn't put a picture of me online, did you?"

"Only a picture or two of you in a bikini with your face cropped out. You're not worried that someone you know might see you on the internet, are you?"

My wife looks nervously at me as she grimaces. "I know that you want to film the sex I have with other men, but that is very risky, Rob. What if someone that either one of us knows sees me and recognizes me? What happens if we are caught doing this?"

"First," I say with a wry grin, "I considered putting the videos that I got from Orange Panda onto the website. I didn't because I figured the men you were with might object since they probably didn't know that they would be on a website. Second, why the hell would it matter if someone recognizes you? If they are watching your videos they would probably be embarrassed to admit it to you anyway."

"Rob, that's just weird." Dana crosses her arms as she looks up from the chair at me. "What if someone I do hair for sees the videos?"

I laugh as I rub my wife's shoulder. "If they do, it would make for some interesting conversation while you do their hair, huh?" Dana does not seem to see the humorous side of my thoughts and shakes her head as she gets up from the chair.

"Dammit, Rob, I'm being serious. We have to think this through before we do anything. I can't afford to have my face seen by hundreds of people with some of them potentially being clients or close friends."

"Do you really think that the people you know are going to be surfing the web for internet porn that includes you?" I say this in jest, but the fact is I intend to reach thousands or more so that paid subscriptions will be the way that I can support us if I were to lose my job at the company.

"I don't know." Dana continues to keep her arms folded as I sit down in the chair at the desk and look at the men in the profile pictures.

"We need to choose the first one," I tell her as I continue to press on with our plan. "You can do this, Dana. Just pick the one that you think would be the best for the job."

"It's not a *job,*" she retorts. After a moment of looking at the screen, my wife tells me, "That one." She points at the screen and I open the profile window to take a better look at the man she has selected.

"Joseph Reynolds," I say as I nod my head. "He seems like a nice guy. He is six-two, two hundred pounds, a university student and athlete." Smiling, I add, "He's got some other nice information here too, honey. Do you want to read it or shall I?"

"Go ahead," she says as she looks over at me.

"Alright. He has brown hair and eyes, obviously, but he has a big cock."

"Big cock?" My wife bends down to see what is written in the profile. "Does he really *say* that?"

"He says a big *package,* but I figured that I would call it what it is," I laugh. "Joseph does not have a girlfriend at the moment, but is open to the possibility. He is very interested in you and hopes that you would like to spend an evening with him." I look down at my wife and say, "Joseph sounds like a solid guy, dear."

Dana scowls at me. "You're having too much fun with this, Rob. Can't you be at least a little serious about what we are doing?"

"I am being serious," I answer. "Look, he's a nice guy and he can probably work you over the way you like to be worked over, right? I agree with your choice, my love. Let's invite the guy over for some sex."

My wife gets up from her chair and walks to the other side of the spare bedroom. "Do we have to film everything that happens?"

"We just went over that, Dana. The website will depend upon having videos for people to stream. I already have people paying ten dollars per month to see you have sex with someone."

She turns to look at me. "Why would they pay that? There are all sorts of sites that are free."

"That's just it," I reply with a smile on my face as I walk over to where she is standing. "There are lots of men and women who are tired of going to a website for generic porn. It's all contrived and not all that original anymore. However, what we have going for us is that this website will only feature pure amateur content about you and your adventures with other men. There will be no other videos of other women, no ads from other sites, or anything that would appear to be just thrown together smut for the sake of website draw. The website is an exclusive site and there are plenty of people willing to give up ten bucks every month for the chance to see what else has been posted for them to watch." Feeling a chill running down my back, I add, "You are the star of this website, Dana. You and whichever guys you choose from here on out will be known by a lot of people."

"Shit." My wife shakes her head. "I still don't like the thought of being filmed, Rob."

"And you need to get over that," I reply. "I will also have to deal with any shit that hits the fan where I work if anyone there sees the videos and figure out that you and I are married to each other. That's why I will not use your real name on the website and you can put on makeup or whatever you want to help change your looks."

"I can wear a mask?" she asks.

I shake my head. "No mask, honey. People want to see your whole face when you suck a guy's dick or when he comes all over it. We have to stay away from the mask thing. I have already looked into that."

"You have *researched* this?" I constantly tell Dana that I am doing research for my website in order to develop an online business model, but until recently I was spending very little time actually doing that. When I discovered that she was having sex with other men on the side and filming the encounters, I decided that it was time to look in a different direction for my online business. This one has already paid out a few hundred dollars as early memberships to the site are on sale at this very moment.

"I have researched it," I confirm. "We are going to do very well with this, my love. Just wait and see." I smile at Dana as I take her into my arms. "I know this is a little scary, but I promise you that things will work out very nicely, Dana. I think you already know that."

She nods her head as she looks into my eyes. "You will have to share the money with me, though."

I laugh. "Oh, you want a cut of the money?"

"I'm serious," Dana replies. "If I am going to do this in front of the camera, I should get something out of it, right?"

"Besides the sex?"

"Of course. You are getting to watch it, Rob. Why should you get the money all to yourself when you are watching it for your own sexual gratification?"

Smiling, I reply, "Dana, it all goes into the same pot, right? The money will be in the bank."

"You know what I mean, Rob. I want a cut of it that I get to spend on whatever I want. That part will become cash and goes right into my hands." As I look into my wife's brilliant blue eyes, I realize there is no way around her request. Of course she is entitled to the money. She will be the one having sex with other guys, not me, so it only makes sense that she has a large portion of the money.

"Ten percent," I say to her.

"Ten? Are you fucking *serious?"* Dana allows a wicked grin to spread across her face. "Seventy-five percent."

"What?" I shake my head as I laugh. "That's highway robbery, Dana. We need that money for bills and such if I lose my job."

"You haven't lost your job yet, have you?" she asks.

"Well, no."

"Then I want that money."

I laugh again as I shake my head. "Okay, honey. Let's be serious now. How about fifty-fifty?" I watch as Dana's eyes narrow as she looks at me. The amount I am offering seems fair enough, though she is correct in pointing out that she is the one having sex with other men, not me.

"Fifty-fifty?" Dana raises an eyebrow. "Are you sure you can't do any better, Rob?"

Swallowing hard, I reply, "I don't think so, honey. I need some of that money to maintain the website and keep advertising optimal. As it stands, most of the half I would get would go into that."

My wife nods her head. "I can accept that." She steps back from me and offers her hand as if she wants to shake. I take her hand and we seal the deal in our spare bedroom.

"Geez, so formal," I joke as I draw back my hand.

Dana smiles. "I would have taken less if you had offered." She tells me this now after we have already agreed to the split amount and it causes us both to laugh.

"So, Joseph, then?" I ask as I step back to the computer. "Should I send a message to him?"

My wife's eyes widen a moment as she looks down at the screen. "Sure. Let him know that he is the one." I watch as goosebumps form on Dana's bare arms. It is difficult to say for certain whether she is being affected more by the coolness of the room or the idea of fucking a young man like Joseph. Either way, my cock is still somewhat stiff as I click on the message tab and begin to compose a message to the eager young man.

"I'll tell him that we can do this next weekend if that is alright," I say to Dana as I type the message to Joseph. "Is there anything else I need to add here? Do you want to tell him any more about you and what you enjoy in bed?"

Dana thinks a moment as she watches me type. "I don't think there is really all that much I can say that will make this any easier," she replies. "If you can think of something to say that would be appropriate, that would be great."

I stop typing and look up at my wife. *"Appropriate?"* We both chuckle as I turn back to the computer and finish the message to Joseph. From what I have read about him, this is a great guy to have over to be with my wife. He is majoring in accounting, so he is intelligent, and he has a clean social media history. The website I am using to select him is a great business model to follow, and I am already thinking about how I can eventually offer services on my own site that will include sexual hookups. For now, I will stick with the videos on demand, though. Dana is ready for the next level in our sex life together and I do not want to do anything to spoil or overshadow that.

Chapter Seven: A Strapping Young Lad

"Come in," I say to the young man as I step to the side of the hotel room door. Joseph enters the room and looks around as he nervously slips his hands into his pants pockets.

"Thanks for inviting me," he replies as he looks over at me. "Is she here?" Joseph has noticed that the room appears empty except for the two of us.

"She's in the bathroom putting on the finishing touches," I answer as I motion for him to walk toward the bed. "Just have a seat here." The young man sits down on the end of the bed and I go to a camera and tripod from where I plan to film the action. A friend of mine in the city gave me permission to use his high definition camera for the evening but has no idea the true reason behind its purpose.

It takes only a few more minutes before Dana comes out of the bathroom with a short bathrobe on. She smiles at me and then at our guest. "Hello. I'm Dana." She walks up to Joseph and takes his hand.

"Joseph," he responds nervously. His body seems to shake a little as he looks over my wife. "How are you today?"

"I'm fine." She sits down beside the young university man. "And how are you doing?"

Swallowing hard, Joseph looks at her and answers, "To be honest, I'm a little nervous about everything. Your husband explained what is expected in the messages he sent to me, but I want to make sure that I know exactly what is going on."

I nod my head at him and reply, "We are going to film you having sex with my wife, Joseph. Then the video is going to be uploaded to a website for streaming."

"Okay." He looks at me and asks, "Does that mean anyone can see who I am?"

"I'm afraid that it does," I reply. "Does that bother you?"

He shakes his head. "Not really. I don't have a lot of friends or family who would pay for things like that online."

"Well, then all should be good, right?" I smile at him as I study the young man. With brown hair and eyes, the six-two athlete is ruggedly handsome and the sort of guy Dana likes to go for. His personality seem to be sweet and unassuming as well, something that I felt was shining through as I spoke to him through the website messenger where we found his profile. Though it could be an issue, Dana has found this quality to be cute and adventurous.

"You haven't had much sex, have you?"

He turns to look at my wife after she asks the question. "I have had a couple of girlfriends, if that is what you are asking. I've had sex, but not with a lot of other girls."

"I see." Dana moves closer to the young man on the bed. "But you *do* like sex, right?"

Joseph looks away and then back at her. "Of course."

"Good." Dana smiles, satisfied that she has a young buck to train, and begins to run her hands along his clothed chest. "I would like to try something with you if that's alright, Joseph." He nods his head and my wife slips into the floor to her knees. I make sure that the camera is on their every move as she begins to unfasten his pants.

"What are you doing?" he asks as he looks at her with a surprised expression.

"Just something for fun," my wife tells him as she gets his pants open and then fishes out his hardening cock. Dana strokes it slowly as the young man's face turns bright red.

"I'm sorry if it's not what you expected," he apologizes.

"What?" My wife giggles as she pulls up on Joseph's johnson and then smears a small amount of his pre-come around with her fingers. She then, without warning, opens her mouth and takes his member in across her tongue.

"Oh, *wow...*" This takes Joseph by surprise as Dana begins to suck on him softly on the end of the bed. His hands remain on the covers, gripping them tightly as my wife slowly draws her mouth up his long shaft and then pushes it back down again to meet his balls.

"Holy shit," I say quietly to myself as I zoom in on my wife's face and the young man's hard shaft. The way Dana is working on his manly wood makes me hard as well and I am forced to reach into my own pants and move my cock around so that it has plenty of room to grow.

"Ahhh..." Joseph grips the covers tighter as Dana goes to the end of his cock and licks around the tip of it for a moment with her tongue. She is probably one of the greatest at giving a blow job to a guy, especially if she likes the taste of his pre-come. It appears that my wife is really enjoying the young man's essence as it slowly dribbles out of his piss hole.

"Fuck." Joseph's body shakes hard as he puts a hand on the back of Dana's head. *"FUCK!"* His crotch lunges toward my wife's face as he begins to empty his balls into her mouth. *"Ahhh...ahhhh...ahhhh..."* He pulls down gently on her head, causing Dana to move down to his balls with her lips and tongue. She allows him to come inside her throat as his face turns nearly purple. *"Ohhhh...fuck...uhhhh..."*

The young man comes for a few seconds before he begins to relax and my wife pulls her mouth away from his pecker. "Wow, that was a lot of come," she tells Joseph as she smiles at him and wipes her face. "When is the last time that you had sex?"

He looks nervously at the camera and then at her. "About two months ago."

"Wow. You really had it built up. You need this, don't you?" Dana begins to unbutton Joseph's shirt as she smiles at him.

"Wait. What's happening?"

Dana smiles. "It's my turn, silly. Oh, and your turn again as well." She rubs his cock with her hand and adds, "You will need to get hard again." My wife gets his shirt off and then Joseph stands up so that she can pull down his pants and boxer briefs. Dana then opens her robe and allows it to fall to the floor, revealing her C-cup orbs of flesh.

"All natural," I tell the young man as I smile at him. "And they are yours for a while." I check the camera again and think about the editing that I will need to do to take out some of the sounds, such as when I say something. We can't have my commentary in the videos, after all.

"Can I touch them?" he asks my wife. She nods her head and the university man reaches his hands toward her breasts. Squeezing them gently, he tells her, "These are more beautiful than any others I have ever seen."

Dana smiles. "Thank you, sweetie." She then lays down on the bed and opens her legs while bending her knees. "Do you know how to eat a girl out properly, Joseph?"

He nods his head. "I have done it before."

"Then show me what you can do, baby." My wife rubs her labia and hardening clitoris as he gets down on the bed and moves his face to her snapper. Dana smiles as he buries his nose and mouth into her folds.

"There you go," I say as I move the camera to a new position and zoom in on the young man's mouth on my wife's pussy. I pre-come a little in my pants as I film him eating her out.

"My clit," she begs the young man. "Run your tongue over it." Dana directs Joseph to work his oral magic on her lady bit and I zoom in even closer to capture the moment as he pulls it into his mouth and sucks on it gently. My wife's back arches as she enjoys the feeling of his tongue and lips on her nether region.

"You taste nice," he comments as his sits up a little and puts a finger into Dana's wet snapper. "Fuck, I want you." Joseph goes back down on her and continues to eat her pecan as he fingers her pussy.

"Oh, Joseph," my wife moans as she plays with her nipples. "You're not too bad at this." She smiles as he continues to work on her muff and I feel more pre-come oozing into my pants from my cock. I wish Dana was sucking on me right now while the young man pleasures her.

"Joseph," Dana moans again as she reaches down and pushes his head away. *"Stop!"*

The young man sits up and looks down at my wife. "Am I hurting you?"

"Get inside of me, quick!" Joseph nods his head and moves his body around so that his cock is against Dana's moist snapper. It takes very little effort for him to slip his johnson into her wet hole before thrusting in and out of her.

"Oh, fuck," he groans as his balls tap Dana's puckered back door. "You are so tight, Dana." His muscular body ripples as he pushes her legs back and lifts her ass from the bed. The university man wants to get deep inside my wife as he works toward an orgasm that will result in him souping up Dana's cervix.

"Joseph...*Joe...*" Dana's body moves up and down on the bed as her lover begins to fuck her hard. She continues to play with her hard nipples as she enjoys him fucking her. "Keep pumping into me. Harder, Joe. *Harder.*" The young man obliges her as he pulls her hard toward him, the end of his cock striking her solid cervix and causing my wife to grimace with each deep plunge.

"Fuck..." Joseph is close to losing his load.

"Oh, Joseph...*ohhhh...*" Dana is the one to orgasm this time, her body tensing and relaxing with each powerful wave of sexual energy being released. *"FUCK!!! Ohhhh...Joseph...uhhhh..."* My wife's hands go down and feel of his legs as they rise and fall with each thrust of his solid pecker. *"Damn! Oh, fuck! OHHHH!!!"* It looks to me like my wife could pass out as she enjoys her orgasm with the young college man

"Uhhhh....UHHHH!!!" Once again, Joseph comes. His abdominal muscles tense and relax as he pumps his load into my wife's snapper. *"Nahhh...fuck...uhhhh...."* Each spurt is powerful even though he has already given up some of his ball sauce to Dana as an appetizer. *"FUCK!"* He pulls a couple of more times hard on her naked body as he finishes emptying himself into her. Then, as if planned, he pulls out of her and drops to the bed beside my wife. I make sure to get a close up of the jism slowly creaming out of Dana's wet muff.

"Holy shit," I laugh as I look at the two of them on the bed. "The two of you together were great!" I smile as I think about the first video that will be uploaded to the website. Just as Dana promised on the way to the hotel, she gave a great show. She had decided that if she were going to be featured in a video, it needed to be something the people would want to see. I can attest to the fact that even I will want to see it; over and over again.

"You were...*wow.*" Dana giggles as she looks over at the young man. "Thank you for that, Joseph."

He smiles shyly back at her. "You were better than anyone I have been with." Joseph, a young man who had very little experience sexually outside of his past girlfriends, has come through with flying colors. Dana is happy and so am I. This video will help us to take off with the website and possible become financially independent very soon. At least, that is my hope.

Chapter Eight: A Profitable Endeavor

"How much?" Dana's eyes widen as we sit on the sofa late one evening in our living room.

"A little more than five thousand dollars," I tell her as I show her the statistics page for the website. "All since I uploaded the first video of you and Joseph together."

"I can't believe that people really want to see that." Dana smiles as she looks over at me. "We could really make some good money with this, couldn't we?"

I nod my head and smile. "We are already making good money with it, honey. All we need to do is keep this going. For that, we need to select your next two lovers."

"Next *two?*" Dana raises an eyebrow. "What do you mean?"

I click on a tab on the website page and show my wife the comments section. "They want to see two guys with you now, my love. That will give them incentive to keep the monthly fee active and maybe it will also bring new members to the site."

"Rob." Dana shakes her head. "Are you sure you want me to do this with two other men on video?"

"You and I have had threesomes before, Dana. We both liked it too, right?"

"Sure we did," she replies. "But you have always been one of the guys in our threesomes. I have never had a threesome without you, Rob."

"You're right. But then again this is something new for us to try for the sake of making a little more money, right?" I smile wickedly at my wife.

"I know you so well," Dana giggles. "You want to see me having sex with two other men anyway, don't you?"

Shrugging my shoulders, I tell her, "Hey, whatever it takes, right? I think that you would have fun with this too, honey."

Though Dana shakes her head and smiles I know that I am right. "Okay, then. What do we need to do?"

I pass the laptop over to my wife after I pull up the website with the profiles. "Pick out two of these guys. They have sent us some additional pictures, including nude pictures."

Dana takes a quick breath. "And dick pics too," she comments with surprise. "I can't believe they really sent pictures of their dicks, Rob."

"They are eager to get to be with you," I reply. "I changed your profile to say that you would like to see fully nude pictures of the men. Most of them also sent pictures of their erect cocks for you to look at."

"Holy shit," Dana suddenly says as she looks at one such picture. "There is no way he is that big, Rob."

I look down at the picture and gasp as I see the girthy manhood on the screen positioned beside a measuring ruler. "Damn. That guy is more than nine inches!"

"He can't be." Dana puts her hand over her mouth as she looks at the picture. "It's not possible, is it?"

"I think it is," I tell her. "Honey, you can't possibly pick this guy. He would tear you apart."

"What do you mean?" my wife says with a frown. "I can take that."

"What?" I laugh. "I'm nearly eight inches and not nearly as big as that dude, honey. He's got a thick one."

"I want him," Dana says unceremoniously. "That one."

"Are you kidding?" I shake my head as she clicks on his profile to bring up a message box. "You can't have that guy in bed with you. He's too damned large."

"His *cock* is large," she laughs. "He's just about the same size overall as Joseph, though."

"Honey..." I become quiet as I watch my wife compose a message to the man in the profile. Though I doubt her ability to take him in during sex, I am turned on by her willingness to attempt to fuck him.

"Message sent," she tells me with a smile on her face. Dana then goes back to the other profiles and begins searching for her next choice.

"You are a wild woman," I laugh as I watch my wife look at some of the other dick pics. One of them in particular appear to be almost as large as the first man's. "Don't do it," I tell her. Shit, honey, you can't have two guys with giant peckers fucking you at the same time. That could be really rough for you."

She looks over at me with a sly grin on her face. "Rob, you are such a worrier sometimes." The comment seems misplaced as I consider how Dana reacted before to having sex on camera with other men. "I'll message him." I look at the penis picture and guess the man's member to be around the size of the other man's. Two big packages are what my wife is apparently looking for this time around and it surprises me.

"I hope that you can do this," I say to her as I watch Dana send the message to the second man. "You have never before been stretched like that."

She giggles as she puts the laptop down on the table on her side of the sofa. "And you are worried that I might get hurt, huh?" Dana places her hand on my crotch and massages the bulge inside. "This says that you are more horny than worried, Rob."

"Honey, that's not fair," I laugh. "I am always horny."

"Oh, really?" She reaches into my shorts and pulls out my swelling cock. "I think that you love the idea that two men with big cocks are going to fuck me hard, Rob. You *love* the idea." Dana bends over and takes my shaft into her mouth.

"Fuck, honey," I moan as I reach down and put my hand on the back of her head. She slowly bobs up and down as she sucks on my cock. "You don't argue fairly."

Dana lifts her head and giggles. "You know you want me to do this. Fair or not, you want to come in my mouth, don't you? You want me to suck on their big cocks too, huh?" My wife smiles before going down on me again, her hand this time playing with my balls.

"Fuck." My body lurches forward a little as she begins to suck even harder on me. I can feel her tongue move along the underside of my johnson as she sucks on me. "Dammit, honey. You are too good at this." I laugh as I feel my balls begin to push my man sauce toward my shaft. I want to come inside Dana's mouth, that much is certain. I just wish that I could come inside her mouth while she fucks the other two men.

"I want them to fuck you so hard that you beg them to stop," I say as I feel myself pre-come into Dana's mouth. "I hope they push your legs back and hit your cervix."

My wife pulls up and looks at me with a smile on her face. "You dirty man. You want them to fuck me hard, don't you?" Dana pumps my cock as I squirm on the sofa.

"Yeah," I moan as she pulls up on my pecker.

"Are you going to shoot, Rob? Are you going to make a big mess?" Dana leans forward and spits over the top of my cock and works her hand over it. She then rubs me quickly with her soft fingers. "I think you are going to lose your load, sweetheart. You are going to spunk all over my hands and onto the floor."

"Shit, honey," I groan as I grind into her hands. "Oh, fuck, I'm going to come."

"Come for me, Rob. Come *hard* for me." Dana smiles and keeps pulling on my erect johnson. Finally, as I begin to breathe deeply, I lose my load into her soft hands.

"OHHHH!!!" The first spurt is powerful as it rises into the air and drops onto the floor between my feet. *"AHHHH!!! FUCK!!! OHHHH!!!"* I move my ass around on the sofa as I feel my sack draw tightly in on itself. *"Nahhhh..."* Each spurt continues to be powerful for a while as I launch my jism all over Dana's hands and into my lap. Closing my eyes, I clench my teeth together and continue to orgasm as my wife catches my white sauce. She continues to talk to me as I finish ejaculating and then lifts her hands from my messy cock.

"You are a dirty boy," she tells me again. "Rob, it's all over the place." Dana laughs as she looks around. "You really want me to have fun with those two guys, huh?"

I shake my head. "I was really horny when I said that, so you can't really go along with what I said."

"You're so full of it," Dana laughs. "I know you, Rob. You want to watch as I have sex with two guys like them. Besides, it will help to bring in more subscribers, right?" Her blue eyes focus on mine as she looks at me.

I laugh. "Well, it should. I wonder how many guys you will be getting off without actually giving them blow jobs or hand jobs." Dana laughs with me as we sit together on the sofa.

"This could be the thing that gets you out of that company, Rob."

"Yeah, it could be. If it works out that way we will have to be sure that we keep everything going on the website to have plenty of subscribers. If we begin to drop our numbers it would mean that I would have to go find a job."

"You could always help me when I open the new spa salon," Dana replies. "You would like that, right?"

Chuckling, I tell her, "Well, I'm not sure that I would be good for doing anything more than just showing people where the tanning bed is located."

"That could be helpful," Dana says as she puts her head on my shoulder. "I just hope things work out for us. If it does, it will mean that everything becomes easier. I hate that place you work for and I know you don't like it either."

"You're right," I admit. "If the website works out I could do that full time and we would be so much better off. I guess we will have to wait and see."

"Along with David and Lance." Dana smiles as she looks over at the laptop on the table. "Two big guys who are about to help us do much better in life. I love you, Rob." My wife turns and kisses me on the cheek.

"I love you too, beautiful girl." I turn and lock my lips onto hers. We enjoy each other for a while as my cock continues to throb from the recent explosion from its tip. Dana makes me come hard whenever we have sex. She will make her two new lovers explode soon as well, whether they fit inside her very well or not.

Chapter Nine: An Intense Encounter

This time feels different than before as I open the door of the hotel room and let the two men inside. "Hello," I say nervously as I reach out and shake each of their hands.

"Hey. I'm David," one of them, a blond-haired man with a square jawline says. Even though I should be more attentive to his general appearance, all I can think about is the cock pic he sent for my wife to look at.

"I'm Rob." I shake his hand before turning to the other man, a dark-haired hunk, to do the same.

"Lance," he tells me with a smile on his face. His pecker is the one that is largest, if the measurement in the picture was correct.

"Come have a seat, gentlemen," I say as I smile at both of them. There are goosebumps running up and down my neck and back as I show them to the bed. Lance has a seat on a chair nearby while David sits on the edge of the bed. Dana is still in the bathroom getting ready for the men she will soon have sex with. I go and make sure that the camera is ready to go as the men make themselves comfortable.

"So, you are her husband?" Lance asks as he sits back in the chair.

I nod my head. "I am."

"That has got to be a little weird, right? I mean, I had a girlfriend for a long time and this is definitely not the sort of thing that she would have ever gone for."

"Mine neither," David agrees. Both men are young, one of them a senior at the university and the other a recent graduate. It was the one thing Dana really wanted to be certain of; that we tried to find other men who were about the same age as Joseph. My wife wants to have sex with younger men because she knows their sexual appetites will be huge.

"Dana is a woman who enjoys the company of other men while I watch," I reply. "You two are the sort of guys she likes to spend time with. Consider yourselves lucky as she looked through dozens of other profiles before settling on the two of you."

"And the threesome thing?" David asks. "How did she know we would be okay with that?"

I shrug my shoulders. "She didn't. My wife decided to ask you after she selected you. It's a good thing that you each are willing to do that for the first time."

Lance laughs. "Well, I have had sex with two other women before, but that was at a party at a friend's house. We were all smashed." He smiles wickedly as he looks at me. "Are you sure your wife can handle two of us at the same time?"

Smiling, I tell him, "She can handle both of you, Lance. Dana is not your usual sort of woman. She has the sexual energy of a twenty-year-old."

"I hope so." More cocky than confident, the young man almost repulses me as I look at him. If I had known about the sort of personality that he has, the complete opposite of Joseph, I would have probably vetoed my wife's choice. As it is, he is here and he will soon have sex with Dana.

"I look forward to this," David chimes in. "Thanks for inviting me."

"No problem. You are very welcome." David seems more like the sort of guy I would prefer to have sex with my wife, so maybe this will all work out after all. It will be interesting to see how all three of them are together in bed.

The bathroom door soon opens and my wife walks toward the bed. "Hello. I'm Dana." She takes David's hand as he gets up and looks into her eyes.

"You are so much more beautiful," he tells her as his face turns pink. "My name is David." He shakes her hand and then holds it closely to him for a time as he looks into her eyes.

"You really are easy on the eyes," Lance says as he stands up from his chair and walks over to my wife. He reaches towards Dana and takes her hand, pulling her to him as he smiles at her. The young man then bends down and kisses her deeply, their tongues swimming in and out of each other's mouths for a moment as they enjoy the taste of each other.

Dana eventually pulls back from him and says, "Wow, that was intense." She giggles a little as she looks over at me. "Are you already filming?"

"Yes I am," I say with a smile on my face. Lance's hands suddenly move along Dana's petite body and disappears into her bathrobe. He begins to run each one over her breasts, massaging and fondling each one as he takes her in with his eyes.

"So soft," he says quietly as he opens her bathrobe to reveal Dana's round orbs. He then bends down and takes the nipple of one of them into his mouth and begins to suck lightly on it.

"Oh, *shit*," my wife moans as I zoom in on what he is doing to her. David stands back a bit and appears to be uncertain about what he should do at this point. Dana puts her hand on Lance's head and closes her eyes as he flicks his tongue over her nipple.

David reaches over and pulls off my wife's bathrobe as the other man is still tasting of her breasts. "There you go," he says softly as he pulls it away and drops it onto a nearby chair. Rubbing on Dana's back, he tells her, "You are so soft."

My wife turns as Lance releases her nipple and she pulls David to her, kissing him. She then tells him, "You are really cute, aren't you? You pretend to be the shy guy, but I can see that there is a tiger inside of you." Dana reaches down into David's pants and finds his cock, pulling hard on it as she whispers into his ear. "You want me, don't you? I can feel it, David. You really want me." She then begins to unfasten his pants as she smiles at him.

Lance smiles as he kisses my wife's neck. "That's hot. The way you are going to take him turns me on." He reaches down and opens his own pants, his cock immediately popping out and touching Dana's ass. The girthy behemoth is every bit as large as it appeared in the picture the young man sent to us in the website message.

"Fuck," David moans as Dana suddenly goes down to her knees and takes his large cock into her mouth. He looks at me nervously before closing his eyes and enjoying the feeling of her soft, wet mouth and tongue around it. "You are so good at this," he tells her as he takes a deep breath. "I've never had a blow job like this before." Dana is able to get most of his nine inches into her mouth as she goggles on his knob. I zoom in to get a great image of what is happening and smile to myself. My wife is so petite that I am getting hard from thinking about the two salami rolls the men have ready to put inside Dana.

"Here." Lance taps Dana's face with his enormous cock. She pulls her mouth off David's pecker and then turns to kiss and lick on it. As she opens her mouth, Lance pushes his cock in and puts a hand on the back of her head.

"ACK!" My wife gags as the large cock enters her throat quickly.

"She hasn't had one this big," Lance muses as he pulls his cock back and then pushes forward again.

"Ack...UTTT!!!" Dana nearly vomits as the large manhood pushes past her tonsils. Lance pulls back again to avoid having her vomit all over him and I shake my head as I wonder what my wife is thinking each time she allows him to push so far into her throat.

"She is good," Lance agrees with David as he runs the tip of his cock over her lips. Dana licks at it as she looks up at him with a wicked smile. My wife is enjoying this challenge, even if she has come close to throwing up from his shaft inside her throat.

"Fuck me," David says to her as he strokes his cock and rubs it on her face. Dana smiles as she stands to her feet. She pushes the young man toward the bed and he lies down. She then straddles him and slowly lowers her pussy down onto his shaft.

"Oh, my..." At first, my wife's tight snapper has some difficulty taking in the young man's cock. His manhood is almost as large as Lance's, so seeing him enter her causes me concern as I consider the fact that Lance will want his turn inside her too.

"Fuck." Dana finally nests her muff down against David, causing him to buck beneath her as she begins to move around on top of him. "I'm deep," he tells her as she leans forward.

"Really deep," my wife admits as she groans. Dana's face is red as she allows his long cock to strike her cervix while she rides up and down his long shaft.

Landon comes up behind her and reaches around, playing with her nipples as he moves his meat along her bare back. "I could come just because of the way your skin feels," he groans as he moves his cock up and down along her spine.

Dana reaches back and massages his balls and smiles at him as she moves faster and faster up and down David's pole. *"Ahhh..."* She whimpers a little as his head slides past her G-spot. "Fuck, Davey." The nickname she uses makes me hard as I watch my wife and the two men on the camera's LCD screen.

"Eat me," Lance moans as he moves around to her face. Dana opens her mouth and eats on the head of his cock as his ass tenses. I wait to see him push his large pole into her throat, but surprisingly he does not. Has the young man decided that there is really no reason to do so? Does he worry that he might cause her to puke all over him?

"Fuck," David moans as his hands grip the covers on top of the bed tightly. *"AHHHH!!!"* He begins to gush inside my wife's snatch as she grinds into him.

"Fuck! OHHHH!!!" The young man's face turns deep red as he comes inside Dana's pussy. She releases Lance's cock so that she can better enjoy the ride on top of his co-lover. *"Ahhhh...ohhhh...uhhhh..."* David's creamy sauce slowly dribbles out of my wife's tight hole as he orgasms inside of her. At long last, he begins to stop thrusting up toward her and instead sits still beneath Dana's petite body.

"My turn," Lance grunts as he pushes my wife down on top of the other man. David's dick just falls out of her hole as Lance finds the opening. His cock is balls-deep in the other man's spunk almost immediately as Dana's face turns red and she begins to squeal.

"FUCK!" With her legs beneath her and her upper body forward, Lance is able to get very deep inside my wife. His balls slam against her labia as he fucks her hard. *"Uhhh...OWWW..."* Lance shows no pity for the woman beneath him as he breaks his balls against her small body.

"SHIT!" The young man moans as he thrusts hard into my wife. *"FUCK!!!"* Lance reaches down and pulls Dana hard against him as he enjoys the feeling of her cervix against the tip of his pecker. *"OHHHH!!!"*

"UHHHH!!!" Dana begins to come as Lance pierces her pussy deeply. *"FUCK!!! ROB!!!"* She squeals for me as I focus on and zoom in with the camera to her small pussy. The action against her twat is intense as the powerful man wedges his monster package into her small hole. *"Ohhhhh...SHIT!!! UHHHH!!!"*

Lance's body stiffens as he begins to come as well. *"MOTHERFUCKER!!!"* He leans over Dana and trusts faster as he releases his man gravy into her snapper. *"Dammit...FUCK!!!"* I train the camera on Dana's pussy to show the sloppy seconds the young man is poking his pecker through. My cock, hard and pre-coming for the last several minutes, throbs as I watch both men's jism drip out of my wife's tight hole.

"Ohhhh...fuck...uhhhh..." Dana's breasts move forward and backward as she orgasms with Lance. She bends down and kisses David's cheeks as Lance finishes inside of her.

Lance soon pulls out of her and backs away from the bed before sitting down in a chair nearby. "Fuck." As he sits down, he puts his hands on his face and lays his head back.

"Are you alright?" I chuckle as I walk over to the young man.

"I think so," he answers. "I just got a little dizzy, that's all."

"Dizzy?" Dana giggles as she rolls off of the first man and allows him to get up. David is wearing his own jism as well as that of the other man. He does not seem to want to keep Lance's seed on his crotch as he reaches for a towel and begins to clean himself up.

"How are you?" I ask my wife as I look down at her on the bed.

Dana takes a deep breath as she runs her fingers over her nipples. "I had a lot of fun." My wife smiles at me as she looks up. "I think I might be a little sore in the morning, though."

David looks over at my wife. "You are a beautiful woman, Dana. Thank you for letting me be a part of this." Though he is thankful for what he had with her today, I get the feeling that he is a little irritated with the way Lance left his spunk all over him.

"You are a fun girl," Lance admits as he smiles at Dana.

"And you are a fun man," my wife replies with a smile on her face. "Both of you were great." Dana stands up and walks over to the bathroom while two streams of jism run down her legs. As she takes hold of the bathroom door, she tells them, "I can't wait to see the video of this later." Dana then closes the door and I am left alone with the two of them.

"So, there you have it," I say as I look at the two of them. "There will be a video on the site soon, and true to my promise you will get a free one-month subscription so that you can watch it."

"Thanks, man," Lance says with a chuckle as he reaches down and gets his underwear. Sliding them on, he adds, "If you need more videos, I can help you out. I even know of a couple of other ladies who would love to join in."

"Um, okay. I will be sure to let you know if we need them," I say as I think how vain this man has got to be. Lance and David both finish dressing and leave soon as I finish securing the video in the camera and breaking everything down. I can hear the shower still running as I walk up to the bathroom door and I think about how Dana took on both huge peckers today. She has not ceased to amaze me as we continue on this sexual journey together.

Chapter Ten: A Proper Business

I wait for Dana to sit down before I take my own seat near her at the small outdoor restaurant. "What's good here?" I ask her as I lean back in my chair.

My wife smiles as she looks through her sunglasses at the menu on the table. I have had the Italian sandwich here before and it was very nice," she replies. "Would you like to split one of those with me?"

"Sure." We call over the server and order one of the sandwiches, split into two parts, along with a glass of water each. As we wait on our food to arrive, Dana asks a huge question.

"Are you going to quit this week, Rob?"

I sigh as I think about the question. "I don't know. How can we be sure it is sustainable?"

"Sweetheart," she begins while laughing. "There are now five thousand subscribers on the site. That is far more money than you and I make together at our regular jobs. You can quit now."

"But," I say as I grimace, "I worry about the future. The site has been active for only two months now and we are still having to work on fresh content."

Dana nods her head. "The subscribers are telling us what they want, Rob. All we have to do is listen to them."

"And do what they want," I reply. "Some of what they want is a little off the wall, honey."

My wife nods her head. "Some of it is, sure. But that one where the guy wants me to scream out his name while I have an orgasm with another man is doable, right?"

I laugh. "Sure. You do know that the guy's name is Bert, right? He wants you to yell *Bert* over and over again." We both laugh together as Dana pulls off her sunglasses and looks into my eyes.

"I can do that, Rob. That will be no problem."

"But the guy who wants you to use a dildo with his image on it to masturbate...wow." We continue to laugh about the requests, but the fact is these requests could be worth some money. When you can make videos that have a personal attachment to the viewers, they are more likely to keep subscriptions current just to see those requests brought to fruition. I am certainly open to do this, but then again some of them are far too crazy to even consider.

"Fucking a loaded pistol. I don't think so." Dana shakes her head. "That one scares me, Rob."

"Yeah, we won't even consider that one. Whoever that is should probably go find a BDSM website anyway." I look over at my wife and smile. "You are a beautiful woman, Dana. Just like the guys have told you over and over again, you are perfectly perfect."

My wife allows a smile as her cheeks become pink. "Thank you, sweetie." Dana reaches over and takes hold of one of my hands. "Are you happy with what we are doing now, though? I don't want to do anything that you don't want me to do."

"I'm good," I reply. "Honey, this has been a lot of fun. Watching you with other men who really want you has done a lot for me."

"Yeah, I've noticed," she comments. "Rob, you are constantly at me now every night. You always want to have sex with me."

"Of course I do," I laugh. "You are the sexiest woman around, my love. Everyone knows this. I have the proof on the website." I squeeze Dana's hand as I add, "No matter who you may have sex with, I will always love you. This is just the beginning, my love."

"I think so too." My wife and I continue to hold each other's hands as we look into each other's eyes. We have taken steps to put more heat into our marriage for each other and it makes me very happy. It appears to do the same for Dana, so that is all that really matters. The money is just a great side effect.

TO BE CONTINUED IN PART 3

Sign up to my Patreon account and receive exclusive Hotwife stories every month and sexy scenes every week!

https://www.patreon.com/karlyviolet

If you enjoyed reading this book, you may also enjoy Hotwife Swinger

[1]

1. https://books2read.com/u/m2rj11

Click to BUY NOW[2]

2. https://books2read.com/u/m2rj11

Sign up to the mailing list to download the *free Epilogues* to Hotwife Sharing Fantasy, The Hotwife Adventure and Hotwife Training and to be updated on all future releases.

http://eepurl.com/c3ICWf

prologue
THE
hotwife
ADVENTURE
KARLY VIOLET
ARLY VIOLET
hotwife
TRAINING
EPILOGUE

KARLY VIOLET
EPILOGUE
HOTWIFE
SHARING FANTASY

Don't miss out!

Visit the website below and you can sign up to receive emails whenever Karly Violet publishes a new book. There's no charge and no obligation.

https://books2read.com/r/B-A-GIXE-PQDFB

BOOKS 2 READ

Connecting independent readers to independent writers.

About the Author

Sign up to my mailing list to receive the two free epilogues for 'A Hotwife Adventure' and 'Hotwife Training' and to stay up to date on all of my latest releases! http://eepurl.com/c3ICWf Sign up to my Patreon account and receive exclusive Hotwife stories every month and sexy scenes every week! https://www.patreon.com/karlyviolet

Read more at https://www.patreon.com/karlyviolet.

About the Publisher

Lightning Source UK Ltd.
Milton Keynes UK
UKHW010813090223
416681UK00002B/527